AKIMBO AND THE LIONS

Alexander McCall Smith

Illustrated by Peter Bailey

First published in Great Britain in 1992
Reissued 2005 by Egmont Books Ltd
This Large Print edition published by
BBC Audiobooks
by arrangement with
Egmont Books Ltd 2008

ISBN: 978 1405 662338

Text copyright ©
1992 Alexander McCall Smith
Illustrations copyright © 2005 Peter Bailey,
courtesy of Egmont Books Ltd

British Library Cataloguing in Publication Data available

Printed and bound in Great Britain by
Antony Rowe Ltd., Chippenham, Wiltshire

This book is for Victor and Doreen

Contents

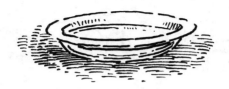

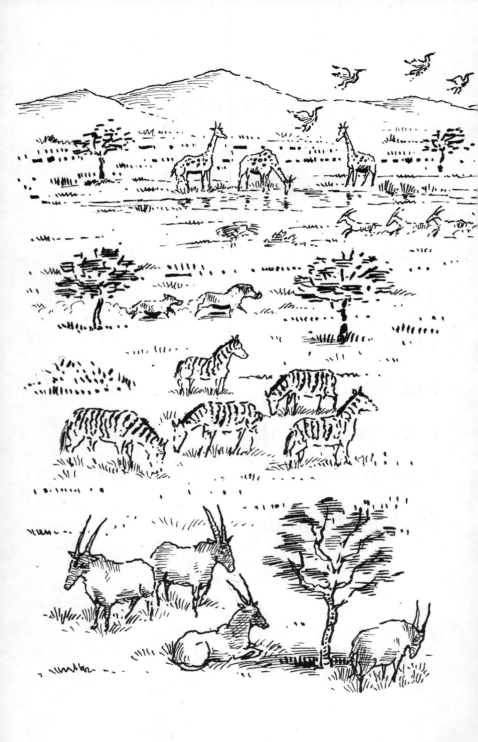

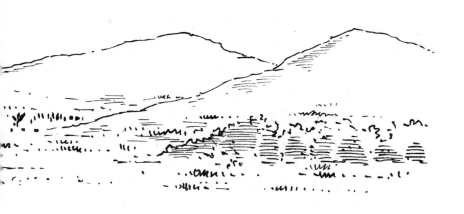

A lion problem

There is a place in Africa where the hills give way to great plains of grass. Zebra graze here, and buffalo too, and if you are lucky, you may also see lions. And at the water holes in the morning, there are other animals to be seen. There are giraffe, awkwardly bending their long necks to the surface of the water; wart hogs, with their families, scurrying in to quench their thirst while nobody is looking; and many animals besides. Akimbo, who lived on the edge of this great game park, knew all the animals well, and their ways.

But now Akimbo was bored. His friends had gone away and it seemed that nothing at all was happening in the game park. His father was too busy to help. He had just been made head ranger and his day was so full of all sorts of pressing tasks there was not much time left over for his son. Or so it seemed to Akimbo.

Akimbo thought about building a tree house. There were plenty of suitable shady trees to choose from, but when he started to look for wood, he found that all the planks which were the right size were earmarked for something else. So he had to abandon the tree house idea.

Then, quite unexpectedly, his father announced over breakfast one morning that he was going to have to be away from home for a few days.

'I'm going over to one of the farms in the south,' he said. 'There have been reports of lion attacks on cattle. They want us to come and deal with the problem.'

2

Akimbo listened carefully. Lion attacks! He stared down at the table, wondering whether his father would let him go with him. Sometimes he was allowed to go with the men when they went off into the bush on a routine trip, but he had never been permitted to help with anything quite like this.

He watched his father, waiting for him to give more details, but the ranger just sipped at his mug of tea and said nothing more. Akimbo decided that he should ask him straight away.

'May I come with you?' he said hesitantly. 'I won't get in the way, I promise you.'

Akimbo's father frowned and shookhis head.

'I'm sorry, Akimbo,' he said. 'I'm going to have my hands full and I just won't have time to look after you.'

'But I can look after myself now,' Akimbo protested. 'I won't be any trouble—I promise.'

Akimbo's father looked at his son. He enjoyed having him around when he had small jobs to perform, but an expedition to deal with marauding lions? That was different. And yet, he had to admit that his son was bigger now, and he certainly knew how to keep out of trouble in the bush.

'Well ...' he began doubtfully. 'You won't get in the way, will you?'

Akimbo leapt to his feet in delight.

'Of course I won't,' he said. 'And I'm sure I'll be able to help.'

'Mmm,' said his father, still sounding a little unconvinced. 'I don't know about that. But I suppose that there's no harm in your coming with us.'

Akimbo could hardly contain his delight. The boredom which he had been feeling up until now had completely disappeared. He was going off in search of lions—the proudest and most dangerous animal in the bush! He had, of course, seen lions in the distance, and on one occasion they had surprised a sleeping lioness only a very short way away from them, but this sounded as if they were going to get even closer than

4

that!

He wondered if it would be as exciting as his last adventure. The tracking down of the ivory poachers and his saving of the elephants had been the most thrilling thing that had happened to him in his life. But it had also been one of the most frightening, and he was pleased it was all over. [*see Akimbo and the Elephants*]

They left early the next day, before the sun rose above the hills. The morning air was sharp and fresh, and the men rubbed their hands together to keep them warm as they waited for the truck to set off. Akimbo sat in the cab with his father, while the men perched in the back with their equipment. His mother had given him a flask of tea and some sandwiches for his breakfast, and as the truck set off along the bumpy road, Akimbo unwrapped his sandwiches and began to eat.

As the sun came up, it painted the plains around them with gold. Flights of birds rose up from the lakes treetops; herds of zebra stared at the

5

passing vehicle before stampeding off in a cloud of dust; an antelope and its tiny calf skittered in panic across the road in front of them. Akimbo had not slept well that night, as he was too excited by the prospect of the trip. Now, as it became hotter, he found himself dozing off, being woken from time to time by a bump in the road, but drifting back into sleep again.

They stopped once or twice before they reached the farm. The men in the back got out, stretched their legs,

and brewed up a pot of tea on a fire of brushwood. Then, at last, just after noon, they saw the farm they were looking for, a cluster of distant buildings surrounded by trees. As the truck drew to a halt outside the farmhouse, the farm dogs barking loudly and defensively, the farmer came out on to the verandah of his house and waved a friendly greeting.

Akimbo sat at the foot of his father's chair while the two men discussed the problem.

'There have been five attacks now,' said the farmer gravely. 'All of them have happened within the last month.'

Akimbo's father nodded. 'Tell me about them,' he said.

The farmer sighed. 'I've lost twelve

7

cattle,' he said. 'In each case it's happened at night. The lion has broken in to the cattle pen and killed one or two beasts. He's dragged them about a bit, trying to get them out, but eventually he's given up and had his meal right there.'

'Has anybody seen it happen?' asked Akimbo's father.

The farmer smiled. 'I put a man on duty at the pen for a few nights, but when he heard the commotion he decided to run back up here. I can't blame him, of course, but it means that he didn't see what happened. He said he thought there was only one lion, though.'

Akimbo's father thought for a while.

'It's probably the same lion,' he said. 'You get one animal that can't be bothered to hunt for prey out in the bush and it picks on a soft target.'

He paused for a few moments before continuing. 'The trouble is that the only way to stop it is to shoot the lion or get it removed. You can't teach them new ways.'

'Do you think you'll be able to trap it?' the farmer asked, sounding rather doubtful.

Akimbo's father laughed. 'It may take us a few days,' he said. 'It may take us a week. But we'll certainly try. And I think that I can say that it'll either catch us or we'll catch it!'

Akimbo swallowed hard. He knew that his father was half-joking, but there would be danger whichever way one looked at it. Still, he had asked to come, and he was definitely not going to change his mind now.

The trap

Later, as they left the farmhouse, Akimbo's father told him of his plan.

'The last thing we want is to shoot the lion,' he explained. 'We'll try to trap him if at all possible.'

'But how do you do that?' asked Akimbo. 'Will you use one of your special darts?'

Akimbo had seen a rhinoceros trapped that way before. The animal had to be moved from one part of the reserve to another and the rangers had shot at it with a special dart gun. The dart had contained a drug which sent the rhino to sleep for half an hour, so the rangers were able to load it into a truck and move it safely.

'We can't use a dart at night,' said his father. 'We won't get close enough

to see the lion properly, and if we had lights it would keep well away.'

'So how will we get him?' Akimbo persisted.

'We'll set up a trap,' said his father. 'We'll put a goat in one part of the trap—lions can't resist goat meat—and then when the lion goes in, the door springs shut.'

Akimbo's father made it all sound so simple. But Akimbo thought it could hardly be easy to trap so large a creature as a lion. Would the trap be strong enough? What if the lion lunged against the sides—would they hold?

They walked back together to

where the men were standing near the truck. Akimbo's father told them to climb aboard again, and, together with one of the farmer's assistants to show them the way, they set off along the farm track that led to the cattle stockade.

*   *   *

All that afternoon the men worked on the construction of the trap. It was made of stout poles, which they had brought with them, and these were dug into the ground to make a strong fence. Thick ropes were then knotted round the poles to keep them together and then further struts of wood were nailed in place. It was hot work under the afternoon sun, and the men had to break frequently for water, but at last, just before sunset, it was finished. Akimbo, who had played his part in fetching and carrying hammers and nails, was pleased that it was done.

'There,' said his father. 'That should do the trick. We'll try it out

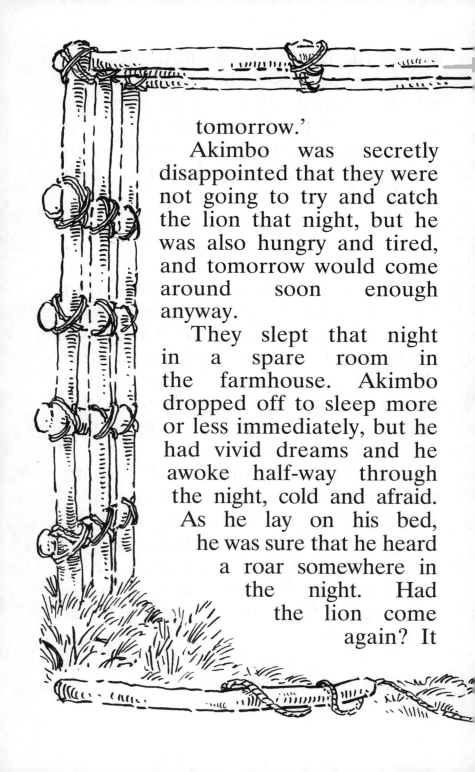

tomorrow.'

Akimbo was secretly disappointed that they were not going to try and catch the lion that night, but he was also hungry and tired, and tomorrow would come around soon enough anyway.

They slept that night in a spare room in the farmhouse. Akimbo dropped off to sleep more or less immediately, but he had vivid dreams and he awoke half-way through the night, cold and afraid. As he lay on his bed, he was sure that he heard a roar somewhere in the night. Had the lion come again? It

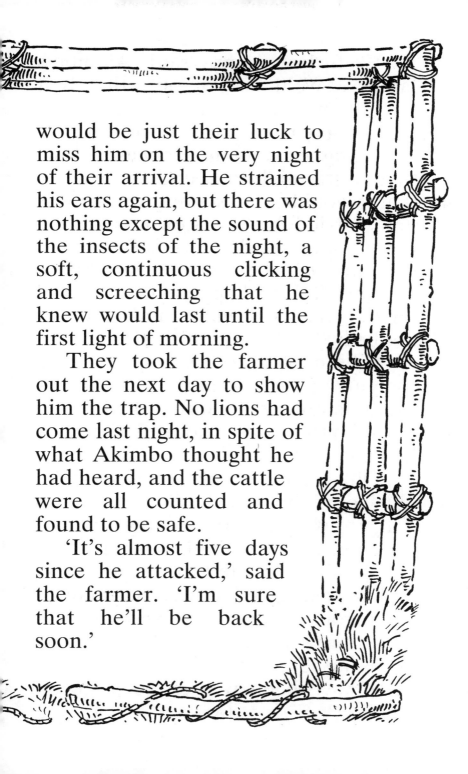

would be just their luck to miss him on the very night of their arrival. He strained his ears again, but there was nothing except the sound of the insects of the night, a soft, continuous clicking and screeching that he knew would last until the first light of morning.

They took the farmer out the next day to show him the trap. No lions had come last night, in spite of what Akimbo thought he had heard, and the cattle were all counted and found to be safe.

'It's almost five days since he attacked,' said the farmer. 'I'm sure that he'll be back soon.'

'We'll be ready,' said Akimbo's father. 'We'll stake out the bait tonight and see what happens.'

Akimbo tried hard to conceal his mounting excitement. It was a long time until nightfall, and he wished that it would come sooner. But he was not worried by the slowness of the hours, only whether his father might tell him to stay in the farmhouse tonight. If that happened, he would miss all the excitement, and he could not bear the thought of that.

'Where are we going to hide tonight?' he asked his father cautiously, once the farmer had gone.

Akimbo's father looked down at his son.

'Oh, I don't think you should be out here,' he said. 'It'll be far too dangerous. You must stay in the farmhouse, as you did last night.'

Akimbo's face fell. It was just what he had feared. What was the point of coming all this way if he was going to miss the real excitement? He looked at his father, and his disappointment must have been written so large all over his face that his father suddenly seemed to soften.

'Do you really want to spend the night out here with us?' he asked. 'It'll be cold and uncomfortable. You won't have a nice warm bed to sleep in.'

'I do want to do it,' Akimbo pleaded. 'I don't want to miss what happens.'

Akimbo's father seemed to waver for a moment before he gave in.

'All right,' he said. 'As long as you keep well away from everything.'

Akimbo was happy to agree. He was keen to see what happened when the lion came, but not at all eager to get too close.

*　　　*　　　*

There was little to do that afternoon, and so Akimbo spent his time wandering about the farmyard. He helped one of the stockmen round up some sheep, and he was given a roasted maize cob as a reward. After that, though, it was just a question

17

of waiting.

At about four o'clock, Akimbo's father hailed him from the truck.

'We're going now,' he called out. 'Come along.'

Akimbo raced over to join his father and the men. He noticed that one of the men was holding a young goat, and Akimbo realised that this must be the bait. He felt sorry for the little creature, with its frightened black eyes and its sad, hopeless bleating, but he knew that if the trap worked it would be safe from the lion. But would the trap work? His father seemed so confident that it would, but Akimbo himself was not so sure.

Akimbo shivered as he thought of it. Perhaps it would have been better to stay in the farmhouse after all. But it was far too late to think these thoughts, as the journey had begun, and whether Akimbo liked it or not there was no turning back.

Lion!

The cattle were already in their stockade when the truck drew up. The men jumped out of the back as they came to a halt and immediately set about the task of preparing the trap. The goat, still bleating sadly, was taken into a special compartment at the top of the cage, and bundled in. It stood unsteadily on its feet and looked about it, wondering what was happening.

It's just as well you don't know, thought Akimbo sadly.

Then Akimbo's father checked the mechanism. It was quite simple really. The idea was that when the lion came into the cattle stockade it would smell or hear the goat. It would be drawn to it and would soon find its route into the maze of poles. Once in, though, it would trip a piece of twine which ran through two pegs in the ground, and this would bring down a roughly-made door behind it. The goat, which was enclosed within a small pen at the top, would get a terrible fright, but should be out of reach of the lion's claws.

Of course the lion could be expected to be angry, and would soon realise that it was trapped. At that stage, Akimbo's father could safely go up to it and fire one of his drugged darts. He could leave that until the morning, though, when they would bring the travelling cage they had with them and could manhandle the lion into that.

'Right,' said Akimbo's father once he had finished his check. 'Everything seems to be in order. Now we must all get out of here.'

'Are we going to stay in the truck?' asked Akimbo, thinking that that would be the warmest place to be.

The ranger shook his head.

'No,' he said. 'That's going back to the farm. There's no need for all the men to stay out here tonight, and it would also increase the risk of the lion smelling human beings. If he did that, he'd keep well away.'

'So it's just us who are going to stay?' asked Akimbo.

'Yes,' said his father. 'But you've still got a chance to go back, if you want to.'

Akimbo struggled with himself. It was one thing to talk about staying out all night in the middle of the bush, with lions about; it was another thing to be actually about to do it. But he was determined now. He would not change his mind.

'No thank you,' he replied. 'This is where I want to be.'

'All right,' said his father, signalling to the men. 'On your way now.'

They watched the truck bouncing away in the distance over the rutted farm track. Soon it was only a cloud of dust, and then that too disappeared, and they were alone.

'There's a clump of trees over there,' said Akimbo's father, pointing to a place a little way away from the stockade. 'We can go in there. That should give us a good bit of cover.'

They made their way over to the trees and found a place where they could sit and where they would be reasonably well concealed from view. Akimbo's father picked up a stick, took out his penknife, and began to whittle away at the wood. As he did so, he whistled a song which Akimbo had always enjoyed when he was younger, and which made him smile now.

'You like that tune, don't you?' said his father. 'Did I ever tell you the words?'

Akimbo shook his head.

'Well, it's about a lion hunt,' explained his father. 'It's an old, old song about the days when our fathers and

24

grandfathers hunted lions.'

Akimbo laughed.

'Would you sing it now?' he asked. 'I'm sure it will make me feel braver.'

Akimbo's father smiled at the thought, and, as the sun went burning down, a great, friendly red ball, he sang the old song to his son. Soon it was dark, and above them a thousand thousand stars appeared in the African night.

'Sleep if you wish,' said Akimbo's father quietly. 'I shall keep watch. Don't worry.'

*   *   *

Akimbo was not sure how long he had been asleep. He awoke, feeling sore from lying on the hard ground, and he rubbed vigorously at his legs to make them feel better.

'Has anything happened?' he whispered to his father, who was sitting beside him, his rifle laid across his lap.

'No,' said his father, his voice low. 'Nothing yet. You can go back to

sleep if you like.'

Akimbo lay down again, but he was far from sleep.

'I could try counting the stars,' he said to himself, looking at the silver fields above him. 'But I'd run out of numbers.'

He thought of the goat, and wondered whether it would be sleeping. Would it be frightened, being out here in this strange place, far from all the other goats? Or would it accept the change naturally, as animals so often seemed to do?

It was then that he heard it, and the sound made him sit bolt upright. The goat was bleating—a clear, sharp sound rising above the insect sounds of the night.

Akimbo turned to his father, who

had also heard the sound and who had laid a hand on his son's arm.

'It's sensed something,' his father whispered. 'We must be very quiet now.'

Akimbo peered in the direction of the trap, but it was only a dim shape in the darkness. In the stockade, one or two of the cattle moved, and then there was a bleating again. It was louder now, with a note of panic.

Suddenly there was more movement. The cattle moved from one side of the stockade to the other, and bellowed in fright. Akimbo strained his eyes against the darkness. He looked up at the sky: the moon was behind a cloud, and it was difficult to see, but then, slowly, the cloud passed by and the moonlight

27

flooded back.

There was a thud, and then, loud and unmistakeable, a roar. A lion was in the cage, and had struck out at the wooden bars that separated it from the terrified goat. Akimbo's father rose to his feet.

'He's in the trap,' he said. 'That's it.'

'What are you going to do?' asked Akimbo urgently.

'I'm going to take a look,' his father replied. 'You stay right here, understand?'

There was a tone in his father's voice that made Akimbo realise that it was no use trying to argue. He crouched where he was as his father crept forward towards the trap. The noise had died down now, and Akimbo wondered what the lion was doing. Surely it would not have accepted its captivity so quickly? Yet he was sure now he could see it in the trap—a large, dark shape, half-lying, half-standing.

In his desire to see more clearly, Akimbo rose to his knees and peered forward. As he did so, his leg brushed against something cold and hard. It was his father's rifle.

'Your gun!' he called out. 'Father! Your gun!'

Akimbo's father looked back. He had not meant to leave the rifle behind and it would be dangerous to inspect the trap unarmed. He turned round, and, as he did so, the lion, who had been watching him cautiously, moved. Unknown to both Akimbo and his father, the trap had not worked. The lion had found its way in, but the mechanism which should have brought the gate down behind it had failed. Then, when the lion saw the man coming towards it through the moonlight, it had lain low, watching to see what would happen.

It was Akimbo who saw the lion stalk out of the trap. He called out to his father again, and the ranger spun round. He was now face to face with a crouching, angry lion, separated only by twenty or thirty paces. There was no knowing what the lion would do, but Akimbo's father realised that whatever happened, he was in the greatest possible danger.

Left behind

Akimbo thought quickly. If his father ran for safety now, that could prompt the lion to attack. If he himself ran towards his father, that could have the same effect. The rifle: that was the only thing that stood between them and disaster. He bent down and picked it up.

Akimbo had watched his father practising with his rifle, but he never used it himself. He knew about the safety catch, though, and he slipped it off and drew back the weapon's bolt. The sound was loud in the night, and he wondered whether the lion had heard it.

Akimbo drew the rifle up to his shoulder and looked down the barrel. For a moment or two he lost sight of the lion, but then he saw it again. It was moving again, down on its haunches, as if circling its prey. He steadied the weapon, and tried to line up the sights, but it was difficult in the darkness.

Then he had the lion in the sights and his finger moved to the trigger. But he stopped. If he fired, could he be sure that he would not just wound the lion, which would then become enraged and take his father within a few bounds.

'Fire!' he heard his father shout. 'Fire in the air!'

Akimbo moved the barrel up sharply and squeezed the trigger. There was a shattering explosion that made his ears ring with sharp fury. He drew back the bolt and pulled the trigger again, reeling from the kick of the rifle's recoil. Then he lowered the rifle and looked towards the lion. It had disappeared.

Akimbo's father came running

towards him.

'Well done!' he cried, gently taking the rifle from his son's hands. 'That sent her off in a hurry.'

'Her?' said Akimbo, still a little dazed. 'Was it a lioness?'

'Yes,' said his father. 'It was. Your first shot sent her scurrying off into the bush, and I should imagine that the second just drove the message further home.'

Akimbo sat down. He was still feeling shaky, and the ringing in his ears seemed louder than ever.

'We'll go over in a moment and see why the trap didn't spring,' said Akimbo's father. 'And I won't leave my rifle here this time.'

'Will we have to try to catch her again tomorrow night?' asked Akimbo.

'I doubt it,' said his father. 'I should think that she's learned her lesson for the time being. Lions don't like to stay around places where they've heard gunfire.'

They walked over to the trap. The goat was still bleating, from shock, they thought, but when they arrived at the trap they saw that it was for a very different reason. The trap had now sprung, and the gate was down, and there was a lion inside. But it was a very small lion indeed.

'A cub!' exclaimed Akimbo. 'Look! We've caught her cub.'

*   *   *

The next morning, when the men brought the truck back, Akimbo's father explained to them all what had happened during the night.

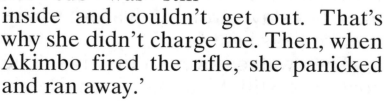

'When the lioness came out of the trap,' he said, 'she must have tripped the mechanism. But her cub was still inside and couldn't get out. That's why she didn't charge me. Then, when Akimbo fired the rifle, she panicked and ran away.'

34

'What are we going to do with the little one?' asked one of the men. 'Can we let him go?'

Akimbo's father scratched his head.

'I just don't know,' he said. 'I suspect that the mother won't be coming back now, so we can't really leave him. He'll die of starvation.'

Akimbo looked out into the night. 'Won't she wait for him?' he asked. 'Don't you think she'll return for him once we've gone away?'

'No,' said Akimbo's father. 'I've seen this sort of thing before. I imagine that she's been shot at by somebody some time ago, probably even wounded—that's why she's taken to going for easy prey like cattle. She'll be really frightened now.'

Akimbo tugged at his father's elbow.

'We could take him back with us,' he urged. 'We could feed him at the house.'

The ranger sighed.

'Who's going to do that?' he asked.

35

'I'm far too busy these days to be spending my time feeding lion cubs.'

'I'll do it,' offered Akimbo. 'I've got the time.'

'And when he grows up?' asked Akimbo's father. 'What happens then?'

'That's a long time off,' said Akimbo. 'But he could go and live in the reserve.'

Akimbo's father thought for a few moments. He glanced down at the lion cub, nestling softly in his son's arms. The little creature looked so gentle and trusting that it was impossible to resist him.

'All right,' he said. 'I suppose so.'

*   *   *

Akimbo's mother was astonished when they arrived home later that day with Akimbo clutching a wriggling bundle of mewing fur.

'A lion!' she exclaimed. 'Surely that's not the lion who's been causing all the trouble.'

Akimbo's father laughed.

'No,' he said. 'But I'm afraid it was his mother.'

'We caught him by mistake,' explained Akimbo. 'His mother left him behind in the trap.'

'I see,' said Akimbo's mother, bending down to inspect the little animal as Akimbo placed him gently on the floor. Then she looked up, puzzled.

'Why would any lioness leave a little cub like this?' she asked. 'What happened?'

Akimbo explained, and while he did so, the cub nuzzled warmly at his ankles.

Then the little lion stood unsteadily on its feet. It looked up at Akimbo's mother, blinked, and then sat down.

'He's weak,' she said. 'Look, his legs are unsteady.'

'He'll have to be fed soon,' Akimbo's father said. 'You should get some milk and warm it up for him.'

Akimbo poured a little bit of milk into a saucepan and then put it on to the stove to heat up. It took a few minutes, but soon the milk was warm to the touch. Then he poured it into a large saucer and placed it before the cub.

The tiny lion looked down at the plate, sniffed uncertainly, and then turned his head away.

'We're going to have trouble feeding him,' said Akimbo's father gravely. 'These creatures are hard to raise in captivity. I'm afraid he might not make it.'

Akimbo shook his head. 'He'll eat,' he said. 'I'm sure he will.'

He pushed the saucer towards the cub again and then pushed his nose down into the milk. The cub snuffled and drew his head away sharply, giving Akimbo a reproachful look as he did so.

'It's strange to him,' said Akimbo's father. 'He's used to lioness milk, I'm afraid.'

Akimbo's mother, who had gone out of the room, now returned.

'Let's try this,' she said, showing her son a baby's bottle. 'You certainly liked it when you were a baby.'

They poured the milk into the bottle and then pushed the teat into the little lion's mouth. He spat out the teat straight away and tried to walk away from them on his unsteady legs.

Akimbo was disappointed. He could see that the cub was weak, and it saddened him to think of how hungry it must be. If only it would realise that the milk was good for it.

'We'll try again later,' said Akimbo's mother. 'In the meantime, let's put him in the old chicken run. He should be safe there.'

They carried the cub out of the kitchen and placed him gently in the wire run which Akimbo's mother used to use for her hens. It was a good place for the little animal, as it was shady and he would be able to move about without being able to escape. He stood up, looked about his new surroundings, and then lay down again.

'We'll try to feed him again in half an hour,' said Akimbo's mother. 'He should be used to his new home by then. By the way, what are you going to call him?'

'Simba,' said Akimbo simply. 'Because that means lion.'

'Simba,' repeated Akimbo's mother, nodding her approval. 'That sounds like a very good name for him.'

Becoming friends

That night, just before he went to bed, Akimbo took a dish of milk out to Simba's run and put it in front of him. The tiny lion sniffed at the milk, just as he had done before, and then turned away.

'You must eat,' Akimbo urged. 'It's no good just turning up your nose like that.'

Simba looked at Akimbo in a puzzled sort of way. He was not at all sure about his surroundings, and he was uncertain whether or not to trust this boy who kept putting a dish of strange-smelling liquid in front of him.

Akimbo picked up the dish of milk and moved it to a corner of the run.

'I'll leave it there,' he said gently. 'When you get really hungry in the night, that's the time you should have it.'

And with that he turned away, leaving the little lion by itself in the run. It made him sad to leave Simba, as he imagined that the little creature would be missing his mother. But he would get used to that—animals always did—and he would have plenty of friends in the game camp—Akimbo would see to that.

The next morning, the first thing that Akimbo did when he awoke was to leap out of bed and make his way as fast as he could to Simba's run. The lion was standing near the gate, his paws up on the wooden struts, and

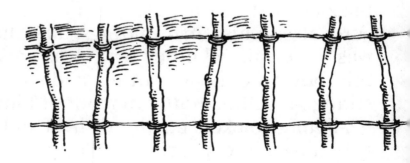

when he saw Akimbo he let out a soft mew of greeting.

Akimbo ruffled his fur, which seemed to give him pleasure, and then he looked over at the corner of the run where he had left the dish of milk. It had clearly not been touched.

'Listen,' he said, as he picked up the small bundle of yellow fur and stroked his back. 'If you don't eat, you'll just get weaker and weaker. You must try.'

But Simba was not interested in the milk, and try as he might Akimbo could not get him to change his mind.

'So he's not eating,' said Akimbo's father when his son spoke to him at breakfast time. 'That doesn't look good, I'm afraid.'

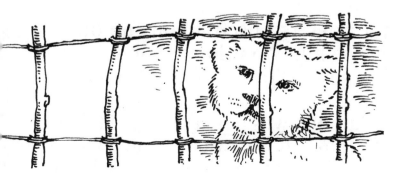

Akimbo's heart sank. He would give anything to get the lion cub to eat, but if he wouldn't take milk, then what hope was there?

'What will happen?' he asked his father. 'Surely he'll get so hungry that he'll drink the milk, even if he doesn't like it.'

Akimbo's father shook his head. 'I'm afraid not,' he said. 'Animals can be strange that way. Sometimes they just won't eat in captivity, and there's nothing you can do about it.'

Akimbo hung his head. 'I don't want Simba to starve,' he said sadly. 'I don't want him to die.'

For a few moments his father said nothing, then he leaned forward and patted his son's shoulder.

'There is somebody who might be able to help,' he said. 'One of the other rangers raised a lion cub once. I can ask him how he did it. He may have some ideas. Would you like that?'

Akimbo was overjoyed. He was sure that there was some way of getting Simba to eat—all he had to do was to hear about it.

*   *   *

That afternoon, the ranger called at the house and asked Akimbo to show him where Simba was kept. Akimbo took him out to the run, where they saw Simba lying, panting in the heat. The little lion was now quite weak, and didn't even bother to rise to his feet when the humans came into his run.

The ranger sighed. 'He's not in good shape,' he said. 'Has he eaten anything at all?'

'No,' said Akimbo. 'Nothing.'

The ranger walked over to Simba and gently opened the cub's jaws. He peered into his mouth, and then felt around his stomach.

'I can't see anything wrong,' he said at last. 'What have you been giving him?'

'Milk,' said Akimbo. 'I showed him some meat, but he wasn't interested.'

The ranger laughed. 'He wouldn't be,' he said. 'Just yet. Tell me—has

47

your mother got any honey?'

'Yes,' said Akimbo. 'I have it on my bread every day.'

'And do you like it?' asked the ranger, smiling.

'Of course,' replied Akimbo. 'I think it's delicious.'

'Well,' said the ranger, 'so do lion cubs. Now you go and mix up two or three spoons of honey in some warm milk and then bring it out here. You may be surprised by what you see.'

Akimbo ran back to the kitchen and mixed the milk and honey as he had been instructed. Then he dashed back to the run, trying not to spill any of the precious sweet liquid on his way. Handing the dish to the ranger, he stood back and watched while it was placed right under Simba's nose.

For a short time the lion did nothing. Then, slowly his nose began to twitch.

'Come on,' urged the ranger.

'Time for lunch.'

Simba had now staggered uncertainly to his feet, his nose still sniffing at the edge of the dish. Then, as if it was the most natural thing in the world for him to do, his tongue shot out and began to lick up the rich white liquid, slopping it everywhere about him as he did so.

'There,' said the ranger. 'That's the end of his feeding problems, Akimbo!'

*　　　*　　　*

Over the next few days, Simba drank more milk than Akimbo would have thought possible. Fortunately, there was no shortage of supplies, as the rangers kept several cows for their own use, but it was not long before Akimbo's mother was sending off for more honey.

'This lion of yours is going to eat us out of house and home,' she laughed. 'Look at how fat he's becoming!'

Akimbo's mother was right. The

skin about Simba's stomach was now stretched tight, and when he walked it was with more of a waddle than the swagger one might expect of a lion. It was difficult not to laugh at him, and it was certainly hard to remember that in due course he would grow up into the most fearsome of beasts. It seemed impossible to imagine that this funny, rolling bundle of lion fur could ever be like the lions Akimbo had seen snarling and growling over their prey.

When he was quite sure that Simba was used to his new surroundings, Akimbo allowed him out of the run. At first the little lion seemed unwilling to leave the security of his cage, but after a short while his natural curiosity got the better of him and he took his first few hesitant steps outside. He was happy to follow Akimbo, and was soon trotting contentedly behind him as he made his way from the run to the house. Every so often he would stop, sit down, and scratch himself, but then he would bound up again, tripping over Akimbo's feet, jumping up at him playfully.

Akimbo felt tremendously proud. It was marvellous to have a lion—a lion all of his own. And he knew, too, that Simba realised that he belonged to him. Each morning, when he went out to the run, there would be Simba, waiting impatiently for his master. As Akimbo opened the gate, the tiny lion would be all over him, licking him and purring, just like a great cat. Then they would play games together, and perhaps go for a walk. As Akimbo walked along, Simba gambolling beside him, he felt that he was probably the very luckiest boy in all Africa.

Lion at school

Three weeks after Simba's arrival, it was time for Akimbo to go back to school. It was hard having to say goodbye to Simba each morning. The little lion whimpered as he saw Akimbo leave, and for a long time afterwards he lay on the earthen floor of his run and pined. Akimbo spent his time thinking about Simba, so he found it difficult to concentrate on his work.

'What are you thinking of?' his teacher demanded. 'You seem to be in a constant daydream these days!'

When Akimbo came back at the end of each day, Simba would leap about him with delight, just as a dog welcomes back his master.

'That little lion has been missing you,' said Akimbo's mother. 'I tried to play with him but he would have nothing of it.'

Akimbo was secretly pleased by this. It made him happy to think that he was the most important person in Simba's life. He decided to teach Simba tricks, and he trained him to pad along beside him when he went for walks. At first he had been worried that Simba might try to escape, but soon he realised that the lion only wanted to be with him and that he had no thought of leaving.

Everybody was very amused by the sight of Akimbo with his lion and soon the story of the friendship between lion and boy had reached towns and cities far away. A reporter came to write an article about Akimbo, and a photographer spent a whole day taking photographs of the two together.

Simba was growing bigger now. He was no longer the tiny, helpless little cub which they had found in the trap;

he was now much larger, and much stronger too. His appetite had increased, of course, and he had long since moved on from the dishes of milk and honey. Now he ate meat, enthusiastically tearing at bones and gnawing at them until every scrap of food had been taken off.

Although he had grown, Simba was still gentle. When he played with Akimbo—when they tumbled down on the ground together and pretended to be wrestling with one another—never once did he allow his claws to scratch the boy. And although he might try to grab Akimbo's leg in a playful way, his teeth, now quite large and sharp, would never cause the slightest damage.

Yet Akimbo knew that sooner or later the cub would become a young lion, and that was the point at which people would begin to ask questions. Simba's run was far too small for a fully-grown lion, and was far too weak to contain him. Would anybody feel safe when Simba roamed the village and began to roar?

*　　　*　　　*

A few months after Simba's arrival, Akimbo had gone to school one day rather later than usual, and had been scolded by the teacher, who believed in strict punctuality. The day got off to a bad start.

It was shortly after the children had had their break that it happened. Akimbo was sitting on his bench when he heard the shouting outside.

'A lion!' somebody yelled. 'There's a lion coming!'

The whole class rose to its feet and

looked out of the window. There, coming along the path towards the school, trotting along with his head held high in the air, was Simba. For a moment or two, Akimbo did not recognise him—this lion looked much bigger than Simba, but when he saw the patch of dark fur under his chin he knew immediately who it was.

The teacher did not know what to do. He raised his hand and then he dropped it. Meanwhile, Simba had reached the edge of the clearing in which the school stood and was looking about him, sniffing at the air inquisitively.

Everything might have been all right had the teacher's cook not come round the corner of the school building at the wrong time. She had not seen Simba, and walked unsuspectingly into the middle of the school yard.

Then she stopped. For a moment or two, the two of them stood absolutely still. The woman seemed to have frozen to the spot, and as for Simba, he wondered why she had stopped walking. Did she want to play? Did she want him to chase her?

As if suddenly pricked by a great pin, the woman screamed at the top of her voice and gave a leap backwards. For Simba this was a signal. So she did want to play after all! Bounding forward, he chased her, soon caught up with her and leapt playfully on to her back.

Inside the classroom the teacher shouted and began to dash for the door.

'No!' called out Akimbo. 'Let me go.'

The teacher tried to stop him, but

Akimbo pushed past and was soon out in the yard. Simba was now standing on top of the woman, who was lying on the ground, moaning and sobbing with fright.

'Simba!' called Akimbo. 'Here! Here!'

When Simba saw and heard his master, he was overjoyed. Leaving the poor woman where she was, he bounded across to Akimbo and began to lick joyfully at his knees and ankles. Akimbo bent down and ruffled the fur around the lion's neck.

'You're not to come here,' he whispered. 'You'll get us both into trouble.'

Akimbo was right. There was trouble, and an awful lot of it. The poor woman was unhurt but she was, of course, very angry, as was the teacher. Still keeping a good distance away from Simba, the teacher ordered Akimbo to take the lion back home and to wait there. He would come across later that day to speak to Akimbo's father.

Akimbo walked back, sunk in

unhappiness. Simba seemed perfectly cheerful, but then he didn't know what trouble he had caused.

'I hope they don't try to take you away from me,' Akimbo said as they made their way home. 'I couldn't bear to lose you, Simba, I really couldn't!'

Back to the wilds

The teacher arrived later that afternoon and went straight to Akimbo's father. From a distance Akimbo watched the two men as they stood outside the game reserve office and talked. The teacher gestured from time to time, moving his hands sharply as if to underline a point, and Akimbo could tell that he was very angry. Eventually they stopped talking. Akimbo's father shook hands with the teacher and went back to his office. The teacher got back on his bicycle and cycled away, glancing uncomfortably over in the direction of Akimbo's house, just in case a lion should come bounding out towards him.

When his father came home at five o'clock, Akimbo had prepared himself for the worst.

'I have to talk to you,' the ranger said. 'I think you'll know what it's about.'

Akimbo nodded glumly. 'I'm sorry,' he said. 'I didn't mean it to happen.'

'I know that,' said his father. 'I'm not really blaming you for what happened. But I'm afraid it does mean that ...'

He paused for a moment, watching his son. Akimbo was looking at him, struggling against the tears, but unable to hold them back.

'It means that Simba will have to go,' said the ranger. 'We can't have a grown lion around here. It's just too dangerous.'

'But he's always so gentle,' protested Akimbo. 'He wouldn't harm anybody.'

'That may be so,' said his father. 'But we can't take a risk. You can't change a lion's nature for good. Sooner or later he might attack somebody. It's in him—right deep down inside—you just can't make him into anything but what he is—a lion.'

Akimbo was silent. He knew that what his father said was probably true and that he would have to say goodbye to Simba.

'So,' said the ranger finally. 'We'll take him out tomorrow and try to reintroduce him to the wild. It would be better than sending him off to some zoo.'

It was bitter news for Akimbo, but he knew that it would be much better for Simba to live his life with other lions in the wild, rather than in the cramped and uncomfortable quarters which he might be given in some distant zoo. That evening, after he had fed Simba, he spent some time just sitting with the sleepy lion, letting the animal nuzzle at him fondly.

'I'm going to miss you so much,' he said. 'Will you miss me too?'

Simba pushed his face against him and gave him a lick. It was his way of

answering, thought Akimbo, and he was sure that it meant yes.

*   *   *

The next morning they set off early. Akimbo sat with Simba in the back of the truck, while his father drove out deep into the reserve. There was a place he knew—a place by a river— where there were several prides of

64

lions, and this would be a place where Simba would have as good a chance as anywhere. You couldn't just throw a small lion out into the bush and expect it to survive—Simba had never been taught how to hunt. But with any luck he would be found by other lions, and some of the females might take pity on him. There might be one who had lost her cub and who was looking for another; it had been known to happen that way before.

It was a long journey, but at last they arrived. Akimbo's father stopped the truck under a tree that grew by the edge of the river and the three of them got out. Simba was excited by his new surroundings, and dashed round inquisitively. He went down to the water's edge and after looking at it suspiciously for a few moments, dipped his nose in and drank.

Akimbo and his father watched as Simba looked about him. He sniffed at the ground, seeming to find something that interested him, and he even gave a low growl. Then he came back, and tugged at Akimbo's shirt, as if wanting him to go off for a walk with him.

'He likes it here,' said Akimbo's father. 'I think he might be all right now.'

It was hard to leave. As Akimbo slammed the door of the truck shut behind him, Simba, who had been walking in some tall grass nearby, cocked his head and looked back at them, as if to say: 'Surely you can't be going without me. Just hold on, I have a little more exploring to do.'

But they did not wait. Akimbo's father switched on the engine,

engaged the gears, and with a rapid turn began to drive away. Akimbo looked back, and for a moment he saw Simba leaping out of the tall grass and looking towards them in a puzzled way. Then he was obscured by the dust from the wheels of the truck and he could see him no more. His friend was alone, and for the rest of the journey back Akimbo felt his heart cold and sad within him.

It was difficult to get used to the empty run at the back of the house, and for a while Akimbo preferred not to go out that way. It was painful to think of Simba all alone in the vastness of the bush. Had he been found by other lions? Had he gone hungry? Had he been cold that night, with nowhere to snuggle for warmth? Akimbo hoped that Simba was all right, but he knew how hard life was in the wild. It would not have been easy for the young lion—he was sure of that.

*   *   *

Several months later, Akimbo's father said that he could come with him on one of his trips deep into the bush. Akimbo was delighted. They would be away for at least two days, and he

68

always loved camping out under the stars.

On the first night they were out, they found themselves not far from the river where Simba had been released. They set up camp that night, below the very tree where they had stopped on the sad day on which they had said farewell. Akimbo's father seemed to have forgotten that this was the place, but Akimbo remembered every detail. He still thought and worried about Simba all the time. Perhaps there was a chance, just the slightest of chances, that they would see Simba again.

In the morning, Akimbo awoke earlier than his father, and he crawled out of the tent to get himself a mug of water from the water bottle in the truck. As he did so, he suddenly realised that he was not alone, that there was something on the other side ofthe river.

He stood quite still, not wanting to give away his presence. The grass and bushes on that side, which were thick and luxuriant, had parted, and five or six lions had come down to the water's edge to drink. It was a beautiful sight to witness, especially since the lions had not seen him and were quite at ease.

Akimbo watched as a lioness dipped her head to the surface of the water and then raised it up again as the water ran down her throat. He watched as the leader of the pride, a large male with a mane of near-black, moved forward to quench his thirst.

Then he saw him. There was a lion, a young lion, just behind the female, and he came forward now and looked at the water. Akimbo knew who it was. He was as certain of it as he could be of anything. He knew in his bones that this was Simba.

For a moment he did nothing, but then, unable to contain himself any longer, he moved forward and called out as he did so.

'Simba!' His voice carried easily across the water, and the lions gave a start.

The male lion roared, and then spun round and darted off into the bush, quickly followed by the others. All except Simba—he stayed, looking across the water at the boy on the other side.

Akimbo moved forward a further step, bringing himself into the shallows. It was not a broad river, and now only a short stretch of water separated the lion and the boy.

The movement disturbed Simba. For a moment he hesitated, but then his natural instincts got the better of him.

'Come back!' cried Akimbo, but it was too late. The river remained between them, and it always would, in a way. Akimbo knew that there was no going back. Simba was where he should be—with other lions—and Akimbo understood that this had to be.

Akimbo turned away from the river and made his way back to the tent. He was relieved that Simba was safe, and although he was sad to have seen him only for so short a time, the fact that his friend had remembered him made him feel happy—and proud.

He looked back over his shoulder, at the river and at the bush beyond.

'Goodbye, Simba!' he called out softly. 'And good luck!'

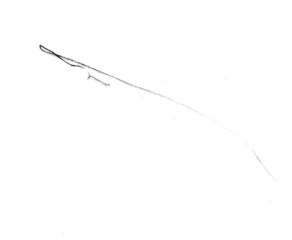